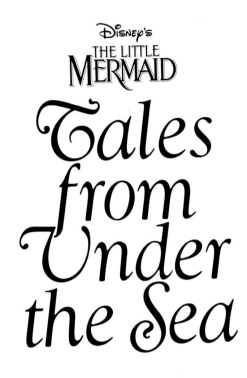

Disney's
THE LITTLE
MERMAID

Tales from Under the Sea

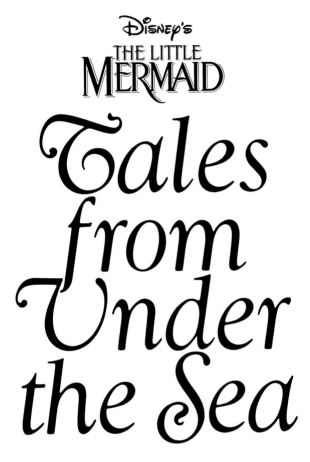

Disney's THE LITTLE MERMAID

Tales from Under the Sea

ILLUSTRATED BY

Fred Marvin

Disney PRESS
NEW YORK

Disney's *The Little Mermaid: Tales From Under The Sea* is published by Disney Press, 114 Fifth Avenue, New York, N.Y. 10011. The story and art herein are copyright © 1991 Disney Press. No part of this book may be printed or reproduced in any manner whatsoever, whether mechanical or electronic, without the written permission of the publisher. The stories, characters, or incidents in this publication are entirely fictional. Printed and bound in the United States of America.

Library of Congress Catalog Card Number: 90-085427

ISBN 1-56282-014-1

10 9 8 7 6 5 4 3 2 1

Contents

Ripples on the Water

Ripples on the water,
Foam upon the sand,
Salty water on your hair,
Seashells in your hand.

Try now to imagine
A world beyond the beach,
Where mermaids play with dolphins
And schools of fishes teach.

Come now and we'll visit
The mermaid Ariel.
About her friends and family,
A few good tales we'll tell.

THE LITTLE MERMAID
FOLLOWS HER HEART

Beneath the sea, in the Sea King's royal concert hall, there was an important little crab who was anything but happy. Sebastian, the royal composer and conductor, had six of His Majesty's singing mermaid daughters on stage. There should have been seven. Adella, Alana, Andrina, Aquata, Arista, and Attina were all practicing their voice lessons. But Ariel, the youngest of King Triton's daughters, was late—again.

"Ah!" Sebastian called out as Ariel rushed in. "You're here at last! We began half an hour ago, young lady."

"Do-re-mi-fa-so-la-ti-do," sang Adella and Alana.

"Where-were-you-Daddy-wants-to-know?" Andrina and Aquata sang as a scale.

"Daddy was here?" Ariel said nervously.

"Yes," answered Sebastian. "And since he asked me, I could not hide from him the fact that his youngest daughter was late, and is *always* late for her singing lessons."

Ariel gasped. "You told him about all the other times?"

Sebastian rolled his eyes. "My dear, sweet, little mermaid, I am a loyal servant and trusted friend of the King. I cannot lie to your father—he's the boss. He was here, and you were not. And quite frankly, I do not know why you cannot be less tardy; more respectful..."

Poor Ariel looked as if she were about to cry.

"Oh, Sebastian," interrupted Arista, "do you have to be so crabby?"

Arista giggled, and soon, all the sisters, even Ariel, were giggling out of control.

"Girls! Young ladies! Princesses! Oh, why does this have to happen to me?" Sebastian wailed.

"Ahem!" A loud voice came from the back of the hall. Sebastian whirled around.

"Your Majesty!" Sebastian cried, and he bowed low.

"Ariel," said King Triton, "it has come to my attention that you have been giving Sebastian here a hard time about these music lessons. This cannot continue.

"I know," said the Sea King more kindly, "that this must be a difficult time for you; you are growing up so fast. But soon you will be sixteen. You can no longer just play the day away."

"I know how important music is," said Ariel, "but sometimes I find myself wondering about..."

"About what, my child?" said Triton, gently.

"Well," said Ariel hesitantly, "ever since I was a very little mermaid I've guessed there is a place above the water where girls sing their songs. I have always wondered what it would feel like to be one of them."

King Triton could hardly control himself. "You are *not* like them, Ariel! They're *humans*! Fish-eating, barbaric *humans*! Ariel, tell me, does your being late have anything to do with this nonsense!"

Like Sebastian, Ariel could not bring herself to lie to the Sea King, so she just hung her head.

"Ariel, whatever you may have heard about humans and their world is nothing more than so many fairy tales. They are very dangerous to us."

"But Daddy, I know in my heart that all humans cannot be bad. When I swim up to the surface and see the clear blue sky and the fluffy white clouds..."

King Triton exploded. "The *surface*! You go up to the *surface*?" The Sea King was so enraged he could no longer trust himself to speak. "Ariel, we will talk about this later," he said, and quickly left the concert hall.

There were tears in Ariel's eyes as she watched him go. She could not

possibly rehearse now. She, too, swam out of the concert hall as quickly as she could. She went straight to a familiar spot, marked by a huge boulder. Her best friend, Flounder, was waiting for her there.

"Let's go inside," said Ariel.

She pushed aside the boulder just far enough to allow them to slide through the opening. On the other side of the big rock was a sunlit cavern full of objects that Ariel had collected from sunken ships lying on the bottom of the sea. Everything that humans made or used was important to Ariel.

"My father is angry at me," said Ariel. "He doesn't like me going to the surface, and he doesn't trust humans at all. He would be even more angry if he knew about all this," she said, pointing to her collection. "But I have such a strong feeling he's wrong about humans, and someday, Flounder, I know I'm going to prove it!"

King Triton

I'm the King of all the waters
With not one, but seven daughters,
So forgive me for a moment if I boast.

But these maids are so delightful,
Never mean, nor rude, nor spiteful,
That I cannot say which one I love the most.

Yes, they're all so very clever,
They say I'm the greatest ever,
And the fish all stop to listen when they sing.

I would give up all I own—
Toss down the crown, get off my throne,
For I know that in their eyes I'd still be King.

ALANA'S GARDENS

Alana was the quietest of the mermaid princesses. She loved to watch beautiful sea flowers grow. She took care of all the gardens around the sea palace and made everything so beautiful that King Triton often brought guests over just to admire her work.

But Alana did not let praise go to her head. It was reward enough to spend her time tending her gardens and looking after all the little sea creatures. She fed minnows from her hands and freed fish caught in fishermen's nets. A turtle she had once rescued refused to leave her side and became her pet.

One day as Alana was pulling weeds in one of the gardens, Arista rode up on a giant seahorse.

"Get up quickly!" she cried. "We have to hide! Ursula the Sea Witch has created a terrible tidal wave, and it's rolling this way!"

Then Arista pulled Alana onto the back of the seahorse, and off they rode to the mountains at the edge of their father's kingdom. In these undersea mountains there were tunnels and caves where the merpeople could hide in times of danger.

Alana and Arista found the rest of the royal family and many other merpeople already there. Within seconds the tidal wave hit. The mountains shook as powerful waves of water poured into the caves, knocking everyone into each other. Alana closed her eyes as rocks and seaweed flew past. Spirals of foam and bubbles were everywhere. The tidal wave roared on and on, and above all the noise the merpeople could hear the evil sound of Ursula's laughter.

When at last it was all over, the shaken mermen and mermaids slowly left the caves to see what was left of the kingdom. Alana swam as fast as she could to the palace. The castle was still standing, but Alana's lovely gardens were ruined! Trees were uprooted—leaving great holes in the ground—shells were smashed, and every single flower had been ripped away.

Just then Alana felt something nudging her elbow. She looked down, and there was her faithful turtle, holding one little sea flower in his mouth.

"Oh!" she sobbed, throwing her arms around his neck. Then she sat up and wiped her eyes. "At least I still have my home—and you," she said, patting her turtle's head.

All that day, and well into the night, everyone in the kingdom worked to restore the land. There was so much to be done. Rocks had to be moved, fallen seaweed cleared away, and sand swept into neat piles. Alana forgot all about her gardens as she and the rest of the merpeople slowly cleaned up.

Finally King Triton came over to Alana and took a heavy shell out of her hands. "Get some rest, daughter," he said, and gave her a kiss. Alana was

too tired to argue, too tired to even return to the palace. She soon fell asleep beside a little patch of coral.

When Alana woke up the next morning she shook her head and rubbed her eyes, unable to believe she wasn't dreaming. All around her flowers bloomed, trees swayed, and shells circled neat little flower beds. Her gardens were back, even more beautiful than before!

Alana saw hundreds of fish, crabs, turtles, and dolphins hovering around her. "Did you . . . ?" she began, still amazed by what she saw.

Yes, they all nodded. Alana's sea friends had spent the night gathering plants, flowers, and trees from the farthest parts of the ocean to thank Alana for all the love and care she had always given to them and to their world.

ARISTA'S WILD RIDE

"There you go," said Arista, patting her giant seahorse's neck. She fed him from her hand, and he whinnied softly for more. "No, Foamy, that's enough," she said. "You don't want to get fat and slow, do you?"

"Those seahorses sure do love you, Princess," said Mackey, the old merman who worked in the royal stables. "You've got a way with them."

"Seahorses are wonderful, Mackey," Arista said, taking off Foamy's bridle. "Sometimes I think they're almost as smart as mermaids!"

Just then Arista and Mackey heard a whinny off in the distance. They swished out of the stables just in time to see a proud-looking golden seahorse speed by them.

"Oh, isn't he beautiful?" Arista whispered, not taking her eyes off him.

"That he is," Mackey agreed. "But a wild one like that would be harder to tame than a tidal wave. I know what you're thinking, Princess, and you can just forget it. No one could ever tame a stallion like him."

But Arista wasn't listening. She was imagining herself riding that magnificent seahorse!

After that, Arista thought about the wild stallion every day. She would see him swimming proudly off in the distance and knew that one day she had to catch and tame him. "One ride," she thought as she groomed the royal seahorses. "One ride and I'll know if I can tame him. But how?" she wondered. "How?"

Then one day Arista thought of a plan. With a large basket over one arm, she began to pick the softest, greenest seaweed she could find. When

she had filled up the basket, Arista carefully set it down under a small cliff where she had often seen the golden seahorse stop for a quick moment before he swam off again.

"Now I'll just wait," Arista said, and she hid, out of sight, on the cliff.

It wasn't long before the water began to ripple and Arista heard the familiar whinny of the wild stallion. He stopped when he spotted the basket of seaweed and then approached it cautiously. Soon he was nibbling on the tender seagrass.

"Now!" Arista told herself, and she darted over the edge of the cliff. She wrapped her arms tightly around the seahorse's neck.

The seahorse was startled. It jerked its head back and whinnied in alarm. But Arista held on and they were off!

Arista had never been so excited. The seahorse raced through the ocean, going faster and faster. Arista saw the blur of surprised mermen and mermaids watching her speed past. She even saw her father, but the seahorse was going so fast she couldn't even call out.

Arista tried to slow the wild stallion down. She tried to pet his neck, to murmur softly to him—all the things her own seahorses loved. But nothing slowed this wild one down. And now Arista was starting to worry. Getting off Foamy and the tame seahorses was easy. You just floated off and swam away. But Arista knew this seahorse was going so fast that she would probably lose her balance and go tumbling head over fins if she got off now. She was afraid of knocking into sharp coral or craggy rocks.

I thought getting *on* was going to be the hard part of this ride! Arista thought to herself as the horse seemed to go even faster and she clutched his neck even tighter.

"Whoa!" Arista cried. But the seahorse did not slow down a bit. Arista and her stallion dashed by an astonished Sebastian. He saw her frightened expression.

"Princess," he called after her, "let go!"

"I'm afraid," yelled Arista as the stallion picked up speed.

"Hang on then," Sebastian called after her. "Old Sebastian will save you!" And he swam to the stables and mounted Foamy.

"Swim, Foamy, swim!" And they were off. Soon they saw Arista heading back in their direction and going no slower.

"Princess," Sebastian called, "can you let go now?"

"I can't," cried Arista.

"Nothing will happen to you if you do. Of this I assure you. Foamy will swim below you and catch you when you go. But, if you prefer, I will take your hand."

"Oh, yes, Sebastian. Please!" And, with most of the kingdom looking on, Sebastian reached down.

Arista stretched out her arm, but instead of being pulled up by Sebastian, she pulled him down!

"Oh, no, now we're both stuck." Arista shouted to Sebastian, who grabbed on to a lock of the wild seahorse's mane.

"Princess, this is very fast indeed!" Sebastian, too, was afraid to let go.

The golden seahorse turned around and swam toward Foamy, who was now below them.

"It is time now, Princess. We shall both let go at once. I will count to three and Foamy will fetch you up at once on his back. One…two…three."

Arista closed her eyes, clenched her teeth, and—let go! And land she did, right on Foamy. But where was Sebastian? Still locked on tight to the mane with his claws. With the eyes of the kingdom on him, Sebastian knew he had to let go. The little crab tumbled over and over and landed in Arista's basket of seaweed.

Nothing much but Sebastian's pride was wounded. As his friends applauded, he brushed some seaweed off and took a bow.

Arista rode up on Foamy. The golden seahorse had disappeared off into the distance.

"Sebastian, are you all right?" she asked.

"But of course, Princess. Just do me a most large favor and do not try such activities again," replied the crab, trying to rid himself of the last of the seaweed.

"But, Sebastian, don't you think a few more rides like that would tame him?" Arista's cheeks were rosy and her eyes were glowing.

"Princess, just one ride like that was enough to tame *me*! The only fast things I am interested in now are the musical pieces I will conduct! I am going to the concert hall for some peace and quiet!"

And Sebastian scurried off, leaving Arista to dream of her next encounter with the wild seahorse.

ARIEL'S NEW FRIENDS

One morning Ariel went off by herself for a nice, refreshing swim. She had just stopped to rest for a moment when she heard a noise behind her.

"Help! Help!"

"Who's there?" Ariel asked, looking around.

"Help! Over here!"

Ariel turned and saw a young merman. His arm was caught in a giant oyster shell.

"I'm so glad to see you," said the merman. "I've been trapped here for hours!"

"How did you get stuck like this?" asked Ariel. "Were you trying to steal a pearl?"

"No, I wasn't," said the merman. "I'm here because of grouchy Old Driftwood. He lives in that cave over there with his two stingrays, Smudge and Sludge. My older brother dared me to go knock on his door and get him to come out."

"You didn't!" said Ariel.

"I can never refuse a dare, so I went right up and banged on his door."

"Then what happened?" asked Ariel.

"He came out, took one look at me, and grabbed my arm. My brother took one look at Old Driftwood and was off like a shot. The old guy brought me over to this slimy oyster, pried open the shell, stuck my arm in, and left me. I've been here ever since."

"Well," said Ariel, "I'm not strong enough to open the shell, but I think I know another way."

Ariel began to sing, hoping the oyster in the shell would listen and be moved by her request. Her voice was as pure and as brilliant as a single strand of gold.

Open up, open up, beautiful shell
And set this merman free.
Of this act I'll never tell,
And forgiven you shall be.

Slowly, slowly, as Ariel repeated her song the shell began to open. The young merman pulled out his arm and sighed with relief.

"Thanks!" he said with a grin. "You're pretty amazing. What's your name? My name's Gil."

"Hello, Gil, I'm Ariel," said Ariel shyly.

"Not Princess Ariel, youngest daughter of King Triton!" said Gil.

"That's me," she said.

Just then, Old Driftwood opened his door slightly and stuck his head out. Eyes blazing, he shook his fist and shouted, "That's it! I've had enough of that racket! Get out of here before I make chowder out of the both of you! Get them, Sludge! Sting them, Smudge!"

The two stingrays burst out from behind Old Driftwood and swam right toward Ariel and Gil.

"Let's go!" shouted Gil, taking Ariel by the hand. They swam as fast as they could, with Sludge and Smudge in hot pursuit. Ariel and Gil swam and swam until they were out of breath, finally losing Sludge and Smudge in a forest of sea kelp.

"Well, you did even better than your brother asked. Not only did you knock on his door, but you even got Old Driftwood to talk to you!" said Ariel.

"Then why do I feel so bad about the whole thing?" asked Gil.

"Could it be because you and your brother were trying to play a trick on a lonely old man?" said Ariel gently.

Gil hung his head. "Do you really think he's lonely?"

"How couldn't he be?" said Ariel. "After all, he lives all the way out there by himself, with no one but two stingrays for company."

"Well, he's still a grouch!" said Gil.

"Did you and your brother ever think that he's grouchy because no one is ever nice to him?"

"Oh," said Gil. "You really *are* amazing. Well, what can we do about it if it's true?"

Ariel thought for a moment. "Come on," she said, taking Gil by the arm.

"Where are we going?" he asked.

"Back to knock on Old Driftwood's door again," answered Ariel. He watched as she began gathering up seagrass, coral, moss, and sparkling shells. She arranged them in a beautiful bouquet.

Gil wrinkled his nose. "That stuff is for girls," he said. "Old Driftwood's not going to like it."

"We'll never know if we don't try," said Ariel.

When they arrived at Old Driftwood's cave, Ariel went right up to the door and softly knocked once. She dropped the bouquet on the doorstep and swam off. A few minutes passed before Old Driftwood opened his door. Sludge and Smudge glided out in front of him.

"What's this?" he said. "A bouquet, eh?" He looked around and saw Ariel and Gil.

"What do you young merpeople want with me, anyway?" he called out.

"We would just like to visit with you awhile, sir," said Ariel as politely as she could.

"That's right," said Gil. "Could you, uh, could you tell us about when you were young?"

That seemed to be just the right thing to say. Old Driftwood's eyes lit up.

"When I was young? Do you really want to know about that?"

"Yes, please!" said Ariel and Gil.

"Well, come on in. Sludge and Smudge won't hurt you," said Old Driftwood with a smile. "They're all zing and no sting.

"Why, when I was young we liked to play tricks on the sailors. We'd knock on the bottoms of their fishing boats and get them wondering what was going on right beneath them! Ha! I've got dozens of stories. Come in, come in!" Old Driftwood ushered the young merpeople into his house.

Much later that afternoon, Gil and Ariel were on their way back home, full of fine seacakes and wonderful stories.

"I'm very glad my brother dared me to knock on his door," said Gil.

"Me, too," said Ariel. "You might ask him to come with us when we go back to visit next week."

And that's just what Gil did.

The Song of Scuttle

A feathery, fluttery
Mess of a bird,
Whose clumsy big feet
Make him look quite absurd.
Is that how you think
Of the seagull Scuttle?
Well, there's more to him
Than just a big muddle!

Now, did you know that
Old Scuttle the Gull
Knows every ship
From its sails to its hull,
That his life has been filled
With adventures and glory?
Well, sit ye, me lads,
And I'll sing you his story.

Scuttle's a friend
To every seafaring man.
He helps us
In every way that he can.
He warns us
Whenever the winds are brewin',
For he knows that a storm
Can be our undoing.

So now to our hero,
Old Scuttle– a toast!
From the men he has saved
As they sailed coast to coast.
Mariners all now attest to his glory,
The mascot of every sloop, raft, and dory!

KING TRITON'S
SPECIAL GIFT

It was King Triton's birthday, and everyone under the sea was preparing for the big celebration that night. The princesses were wrapping presents and decorating the palace, the royal chef was baking a special cake, and Sebastian was rehearsing the Crustacean Band. He had composed a new song in honor of His Majesty, but Minnow just couldn't keep time with the others. The band was getting tired.

"I give up!" Minnow finally said, folding his fins stubbornly. "I'm just too young to be a good musician."

"So you think that if you're young you can't do things, do you, Minnow?" Sebastian asked. "Where would all of us be today if King Triton had felt that way?"

"What do you mean, Sebastian?" Minnow asked.

"Don't you know?" Sebastian asked in surprise. He looked around. "Don't any of you know the story of King Triton and the Sea Witch?"

Everyone in the band shook his head.

"Well, then it's time you heard," Sebastian said.

"Many years ago, Ursula the Sea Witch ruled the kingdom. She lived in the palace and forced all the mermen and mermaids to be her slaves. Oh, she was cruel, that one. She thought she knew more about the ocean than anyone. Well, she was wrong.

"Now, Triton was a very young man when Ursula ruled, but even so, he was determined to free all the merpeople. Everyone told him there was nothing he could do. He was not even a full-grown merman, and Ursula was the most powerful witch of all. But Triton was determined and he had an idea.

"Triton began to tell everyone that he had found a pirate's treasure chest buried at the bottom of the sea. He claimed it was filled with diamonds and emeralds and rubies and gold—more riches than anyone could imagine. One day Ursula, too, heard this young merman boast that his treasure was worth far more than all of the riches in the royal castle combined.

"This was more than Ursula could stand. She sent for Triton and demanded to know where this wonderful treasure was. He didn't want to tell her, but when Ursula threatened to imprison him, Triton agreed to take her to it. They swam far away to a gloomy, dark cave. Deep inside there was a treasure chest, half-covered with sand.

"'I'm going to stand back now,' Triton said, and he moved toward the mouth of the cave. 'The bright light flashing from the jewels hurts my eyes.'

"Ursula did not even pay any attention to him. She quickly threw open the lid to the chest. But there was no treasure inside, only the evil Undertow, which pulled her into the chest and down, down, down to the deepest, blackest depths of the ocean. It would take her many, many years to swim her way back.

"Triton quickly returned to the kingdom. When the mermen and mermaids heard what he had done, they all declared him king. And that is how King Triton came to rule the seas."

The fishes were silent for a moment. Then Minnow spoke. "If a young merman is smart enough to conquer the Sea Witch," he said, "I guess a young fish like me can keep time in an orchestra."

The band began to practice again, with a new energy. That night, when the Crustacean Band played their new piece, the King was so pleased he congratulated each member of the band personally. Minnow had never been so proud as when he bowed before the greatest merman in the kingdom.

ANDRINA'S PERFORMANCE

Andrina was the most athletic of all of King Triton's daughters. She won all the trophies for underwater sports, loved playing catch with the mermen, and was always practicing aerobics around the palace. In fact, she was very often swimming or tumbling when she should have been studying literature or history or music. Andrina could simply not sit still long enough to enjoy her studies.

This was a problem for Sebastian. Music and singing were an important part of a royal mermaid's education, and he often had to chase after Princess Andrina to get her to practice her singing. But Andrina's voice was as lovely as those of her sisters. Her singing was so pure and clear Sebastian felt it was well worth the chase.

One morning, as all seven mermaid sisters were practicing their scales, Sebastian had an announcement to make.

"As King Triton's entrusted, humble servant," he began regally, "it is my great privilege to compose a special tribute to His Royal Highness. And I have decided that each of you princesses will sing a piece of your own composition to honor your father."

"Oh, Sebastian!" Ariel cried, clapping her hands. "What a wonderful idea!"

"Can I sing first?" begged Adella.

"I'll pick some flowers for all of us to wear in our hair for the concert," said Alana dreamily.

Aquata, Arista, and Attina began trying out verses at once.

Only Andrina was silent. Compose a piece of music? Add words? She

felt she could never do that. She could barely sit still to sing the words Sebastian handed to her.

"I can't do it," she said.

"Oh, Andrina," said Ariel. "What's the matter? Don't you want to sing for Daddy?"

"Of course I do," Andrina said. "But I can't write my own piece. I'm no good at that sort of thing."

"But you have to!" Adella cried. "It won't be right if everybody sings except you!"

Andrina didn't know what to say, so she swam off by herself.

During the next few days, the whole palace rang with the happy voices of the little mermaids as they tried out the songs they had written. Sebastian had never seen the princesses work so hard.

Only Andrina had yet to write something. She couldn't concentrate. Every time she sat down, she had to get up. What if she did write something and it wasn't any good? What if everyone laughed at her? It was too terrible to think about.

Sebastian was getting worried. The concert was quickly approaching, and he knew King Triton would be very disappointed if Andrina did not perform her own piece. He decided it was time to have a talk with her.

"Andrina, I just don't understand you," he began. "You haven't even written a line. Aren't you trying?"

"But Sebastian, I do try. I'm just no good at this sort of thing," said Andrina.

"Well, if you keep jumping up and rushing off you'll never write anything. Don't you realize, Princess," said Sebastian, "that as long as the piece is from you, your father cannot help but like it?"

But say what he might, Sebastian could not get Andrina to write a single note of music.

The night of the concert arrived and six mermaid sisters eagerly swam to the concert hall, ready to perform their original works. Andrina stayed behind.

"I don't know why it's so easy for Ariel and the others to write music for Daddy," she said, sighing. "Well, it would be another story if they had to race seahorses for him, or swim in competition, or..." A smile began to spread across Andrina's face. She knew just what to do as a tribute for her father.

Andrina swam quickly to the concert hall and whispered a few words to Sebastian before taking her seat. Her sisters were delighted but very puzzled. What would Andrina do? When her turn came, Sebastian signaled the band to play the Sea King's favorite song, and while Andrina sang it, she gave the audience the best acrobatics show they had ever seen! And King Triton loved every minute of it, too, since he knew Andrina's act came straight from the mermaid's heart.

Under the Ocean

Under the ocean,
There was quite a commotion,
When two mermaids went out to play.

A seashell they spied,
"It's mine!" they each cried,
As each shoved the other away.

They started to fight.
Soon the seashell got buried
Away out of sight.

A lesson was learned,
And so homeward they turned,
Ashamed of what they had done.

For it's better to share
When there's only one there,
And selfishness spoils the fun.

A D E L L A   A N D
T H E   P I N K   P E A R L

Princess Adella loved to look at herself in the mirror. She believed she was the ocean's most beautiful mermaid and would tell that to anyone who cared to listen. Her sisters did not care to listen. Adella told them anyway.

One evening, Adella had a date with a most handsome young merman and she was having trouble deciding what to wear.

"Should I wear the green or the pink?" she asked her sisters. "Both look divine on me; it's so hard to choose."

"Oh, brother," said Ariel.

Adella turned to the mirror. She held her hair up, then let it down. Up. Down. Up. Down. "Which do you think is more stunning?" she asked.

"For heaven's sake, Adella!" said Aquata.

Adella opened her jewel box. She looked through it and held up a pearl necklace. "Well, I'm sick of this old thing," she said. "Have any of you got a *pink* pearl?"

"A pink pearl!" said Attina. "Oh, Adella, you know how impossible it is to find one of those."

"But I *want* one!" Adella insisted. "And I always get what I want!" And with that, she swam away.

"Someday Adella's vanity will make her go too far," said Ariel. Her sisters nodded in agreement.

Adella headed for the twisting dark caverns that led to oyster beds hardly ever visited by anyone in the kingdom. She thought she'd have more of a chance of finding a pink pearl if she went where other merpeople wouldn't

go. What she had forgotten was how dark and deserted a place she was entering.

She shrugged off her fear. I'm a princess, after all, she thought. What harm could possibly come to me?

Finally Adella came to a clearing where she found an oyster bed. She traveled from one oyster to another, searching for her treasure. She scoffed at the dozens of white pearls she passed. These are for ordinary merpeople, she thought.

She came, at last, upon an oyster with a perfect pink pearl nestled in its velvety center.

Adella stared at the pearl. It was magnificent, worthy of her. She began to talk to herself out loud about how wonderful the pearl would look in her hair that night, how this date would surely fall in love with her as quickly as had all her previous dates, how there was no one who would look as beautiful as she, and so on.

She did not notice that as she spoke, one by one the oysters closed their shells and seemed to sleep. Finally she reached in to take her pearl and go. Just then, the oyster let out a great snore and closed its shell, trapping Adella by the wrist.

"Hey!" she cried in surprise. "Let me go!"

But the ugly brown oyster did not budge.

"Pleeease let me go," she said, making her voice as sweet as she could.

Still the oyster did not budge.

Adella looked around. She was alone, surrounded only by bumpy oysters. Shadows seemed to be moving in the dark, cold water. And worst of all, no one really knew where she was. Adella began to get scared. She continued to talk, this time not quite so confidently.

"Did you hear that I'm a princess?" she asked the oyster. "My father is King Triton, and I am the most beautiful of his seven daughters. Wouldn't you like to help someone as important as I?"

The oyster snored loudly.

"I said," wheedled Adella, her voice getting a little higher, "wouldn't you be honored to free the most beautiful daughter of King Triton?"

But the oyster didn't move.

Finally Adella lost her temper.

"Open up, you ugly, slimy thing! How dare you hold me this way, you beastly, smelly creature! I deserve that pearl more than you do! I'm beautiful and graceful and a princess besides! You're just an icky, mossy shell!" she shrieked, pounding her fist on the top of the oyster and swishing her tail furiously.

But there was no response. Adella slumped down beside the oyster. How would she ever be found in time for her date, in time for her to do her hair and find the perfect outfit?

As Adella sat quietly, the oysters around her slowly began to open their shells. She looked hopefully at the oyster that held her. Slowly, slowly, it opened its shell, too, freeing Adella's wrist.

"Well, it's about time," said Adella. "You obviously don't realize who you are dealing with—"

"On the contrary," interrupted the oyster. "I know very well who I'm dealing with. A spoiled, vain princess who puts us all to sleep with her tiresome talk about herself. And I'm warning you, if you keep it up, I'm very likely to fall asleep again with my pearl inside me. So, little princess, if you want the pearl, take it, but be quiet and go!"

Adella had never had anyone speak to her this way. She was truly speechless, but she grabbed the pearl and began to swim away. Then she stopped, turned back, and carefully placed the pearl back where she had found it.

"You know, you've already given me a pearl," she said, "a pearl of wisdom, that I hope I will carry with me longer than I might have worn your pink pearl. Thank you." She ducked her head and swam off, eager to get ready for her date—with her old pearl necklace, which suddenly seemed quite lovely to her after all.

Fishy Holiday

Come one, come all,
In lake and pond,
In rivers flowing,
And beyond.
Little fishies come and play,
It's a splishy-splashy day!

Crystal streams,
And oceans deep,
Wake up fishies!
Do not sleep!
All the fishies shout "Hurray!"
It's a Fishy Holiday!

FISH
SCHOOL

CLOSED

A FISH OUT OF WATER

One day Flounder was busy playing with his friends when they began to talk about how far they had swum.

"Once I swam all the way to the underwater volcano!" said Swishy.

"Oh, that's nothing," boasted Fantail. "I do that all the time."

"Well, just yesterday I swam all the way to the coral reef and back!" gloated Snorkel.

One by one the fish tried to top each other in their tales of far-flung adventures. All except Flounder, that is. He was thinking how nice it was right here, in this little part of the sea, with its familiar places, his fish friends, Ariel and her sisters, and even crusty old Sebastian. He really didn't want to travel anywhere very far away. He liked home. But before he could think of how to explain this to his friends— SWOOSH!—he felt himself being scooped up out of the water and carried high above the sea. Flounder was in the beak of a big pelican!

"Hey!" he shouted as loudly as he could. "Put me down! Put me down!" But when he looked over the side of the pelican's beak, he was glad the bird was ignoring him. It looked like a looong way down. Finally the big bird flew down, down, down, and—PLOP!—Flounder was dropped into a little tidal pool.

The water felt so good on Flounder's scales that he splashed around happily for a few minutes while the pelican just watched him. Then he turned to the big bird and said, "Say, what's the big idea?"

But all the pelican said was, "I'm sorry if I've inconvenienced you, but now I've got to find my babies." And with a loud flap of her wings, she

was back in the air, soaring higher and higher.

"Take me home!" yelled Flounder, but he knew the pelican couldn't hear him. "What in the world could she want with me?" Flounder wondered. He decided he would ask Scuttle what birds want with fish when he got back home.

Swimming around in the tidal pool was lonely and boring. Flounder was glad when he heard voices coming, but when he looked up he gasped.

Humans! There were two little boys looking right down at Flounder!

All Flounder could think about were the terrible things he had heard about humans from everyone under the sea. Everyone, of course, but Ariel. During the hours Ariel and Flounder spent in her grotto with all her man-made treasures, Ariel spoke to Flounder about her hopes and dreams about human beings.

Flounder forced himself to think about the things Ariel had said. He smiled hopefully up at the two boys.

"Let's take him with us," said one boy to the other. And he leaned forward and scooped Flounder up in a pail.

Flounder tried not to be scared. He kept thinking that if Ariel liked humans, well, they couldn't all be that bad. He just wished he could go back home.

"Time to go, boys!" Flounder heard a voice call. "Hooray," he thought. "Now the boys will put me back in the ocean and I'll swim back to my friends."

But Flounder never heard the wonderful splash of his hitting the water. Instead he felt a thud. The boys had emptied the pail right on the street. And now they were pushing him down a hole.

"This is terrible!" said Flounder. "How will I get back to the sea now?"

SPLASH! Flounder opened his eyes. He was back in the water! It was a dark, narrow waterway, but it was water.

"I hope this is a good sign!" sighed Flounder.

He swam this way and that, looking for a way back to the sea. He raised his head above the water to have a look around and found himself face to face with a little gray mouse.

"Oh, please don't hurt me!" he begged when he saw the mouse's sharp white teeth.

"Calm down," said the mouse. "I'm not going to hurt you! I live down here."

"Really?" said Flounder. "Do you know which way I go to find the sea?"

"Go straight down this way and make a left. You'll know you're almost there when the water gets salty," the mouse said.

Flounder thanked the mouse and swam off as quickly as he could. When he could taste and smell the salty water, he swam even faster. He was too excited to be going home to even think he was tired.

"Flounder, you're safe!" Minnow cried when he saw his friend. "What happened? Where have you been?" Flounder told everyone the whole story.

"Humans," said Swishy. "You were with humans."

"Land," said Fantail. "You've been on land."

They all looked at their friend with deep respect. All their long swims could not compare with Flounder's dangerous journey.

"What a story this will make to tell your grandchildren!" said Snorkel.

Flounder just smiled. He wasn't sure he'd want to remember this day. It had been too full of adventure for his taste. He knew that one day he would be more than happy to tell his grandchildren about his friends and his adventures under the sea, where he belonged. But for right now, this tired little fish wanted a nice, long nap!

SCUTTLE'S UNDERWATER ADVENTURE

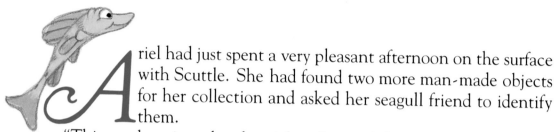

Ariel had just spent a very pleasant afternoon on the surface with Scuttle. She had found two more man-made objects for her collection and asked her seagull friend to identify them.

"This one here is a whatchamightcallit, and this other one, why it's a howdydoodle!"

Ariel sighed. "Scuttle, you know everything about humans. How do you do it?"

"It's simple, Princess," answered Scuttle, holding up a wing. "You can do whatever you put your mind to, you know." He slipped off his rock, but before he landed in the water, Ariel pushed him back up.

"I hope you're right, Scuttle," said Ariel, "because I have a mind to do a lot of things. But now I have to go." And with a quick peck on his beak and a little splash, Ariel was gone.

"So long, Princess," said Scuttle, and he looked around. This was always happening. His friends were always going back under the sea. Of course, that's where they lived, but a seagull could get lonely when his friends were fish and mermaids.

Gee, I'd like to know what goes on down there, thought Scuttle. "What was that I just told Ariel—brush after every meal? No. Neither a borrower nor a lender be? No, no, that's not it." Scuttle wrinkled his brow.

"I've got it!" he squawked, and almost slipped off his rock again. "You can do whatever you put your mind to." He nodded, pleased at his excellent memory.

"Now, why did I think that up again?" He scratched his head.

"Oh, yeah. I'd like to go under the sea and visit Ariel, and maybe if I close my eyes and put my mind to it, I can get there."

Scuttle squeezed his eyes shut. Sure is dark in here, he thought.

Scuttle thought and thought about what it must be like under the sea. He started to picture life under the water....

"Scuttle, what are you doing here?" asked Ariel in amazement.

Scuttle opened his eyes to find himself under the sea!

"I, er, I put my mind to it to see what it would be like to live under the ocean...so, er, here I am," said Scuttle, who was very pleased with himself and more than a little surprised.

Scuttle was having no trouble breathing. He was having no trouble seeing, either, thanks to the goggles he had brought along. He decided to try swimming. He used his wings as fins and his feet as flippers, but he had a hard time doing both at once.

"Swimming is pretty difficult," Scuttle mumbled.

Ariel thought Scuttle looked very funny, but she tried not to laugh. "You'll get the hang of it," she said. "Let's go find Flounder."

"Scuttle!" shouted Flounder when he saw his friends. "This is amazing. Wow, you're just like a fish—a birdfish!"

"Come with us, little buddy," Scuttle said to Flounder. "Ariel is going to show me around."

So the three friends went on their way. Scuttle was having trouble swimming, but he kept going. His eyes were wide open in wonder. How beautiful everything was!

"Ariel," he said, "there are more colors down here than on all the boats we've watched put together!"

Scuttle, Ariel, and Flounder swam to a coral reef where they played for a while. Scuttle picked up a large pink-and-white shell and held it to his ear. "I can hear the ocean," he said with a look of wonder. Ariel and Flounder giggled.

Next they swam past the palace and its gardens. "Nice little house you have there, Princess." Scuttle whistled in awe as they swam by.

As they passed the royal stables, Ariel asked, "Are you tired, Scuttle? Do you want to ride a seahorse?"

"Thank you, but no, Princess," said Scuttle. "I might get seasick! As a matter of fact, my wings are kind of pooped. I think I'll rest on this rock for a minute."

Ariel and Flounder went to swim nearby.

Suddenly, Scuttle sat straight up. It felt like his rock was moving.

"Oh, boy! I think I need some help here!" cried Scuttle.

Suddenly Scuttle *was* moving, and very fast. He wasn't on a rock at all—he was on a whale!

"Swim off, Scuttle! Swim off!" cried Ariel, but her friend was too scared. He held on to the whale's back and closed his eyes. The whale didn't know he was carrying a passenger and he went at top speed through the coral and seaweed. Scuttle's whole body shook up and down, and then he lost his grip. Forgetting he could swim, he slipped off the whale's back and landed on the ocean floor. He had a long way to swim back to his friends.

"Princess," said Scuttle when he reached them, "it's been great to visit you here, but I'm waterlogged. I've got to get back to my little island and dry out. See you."

Scuttle summoned the rest of his strength and swam upward. He climbed onto his rock, and back in the warm sun, he fell asleep instantly.

When he awoke the next morning, Scuttle stretched and yawned and said, "Boy, what a strange dream I had." Then he looked down and saw a strand of seaweed wound around his foot. "It was a dream, wasn't it?" And Scuttle put his mind to asking Ariel as soon as he saw her.

Sebastian's Frustration

As King Triton's court musician,
I write music on commission,
So we'll play a composition
Of my own.

I must ask you to be seated,
For King Triton has decreed it,
And just once I will repeat it—
Please sit down!

Yes, I see you're all excited,
And I'm sure that I'll be knighted,
For the king will be delighted
When we play.

What, your xylophone needs tuning?
And the bassoonists are all swooning?
And the tuna fish is crooning?
Why today?

Though this royal occupation
Is a life full of frustration,
To be Number One Crustacean
I persist.

So, please no more be delayers,
You're King Triton's famous players!
Oh, I don't know what the use is—
You're dismissed!

SEBASTIAN'S NEW OVERCOAT

"Hmmm," said Sebastian, staring into his closet. "What can I wear for the concert tonight? We are playing so many new pieces I do believe a new shell overcoat is in order."

Sebastian went out and began to look carefully at the ocean floor.

"It must be dignified," he said, "but with a little flair." Just then a shell caught his eye. "Why, the ladies will all swoon when they see me in this," he said, chuckling to himself. It was a very fine shell indeed—shiny pink on the inside, creamy white on the outside.

Sebastian tried it on. It fit splendidly over his own shell.

As Sebastian walked home, he began to hear a roaring sound. It felt as if the sound were all around him. Sebastian looked around, but he could see nothing. Then he saw Ariel and Flounder picking sea anemones.

Sebastian stopped and called to the princess. "Are you making that dreadful noise?"

Ariel looked up. "What noise?" she asked.

"Why, that rushing sound," said Sebastian. "It's…it's…why, it's stopped. How do you like my new overcoat for tonight's concert, Princess?" As Sebastian turned to model his new shell for Ariel, the noise began again. He stopped. The noise stopped. He turned. The noise came back. He stopped again. No noise.

"What a crazy coat!" cried Sebastian as he quickly took off the shell and tossed it down.

Ariel and Flounder laughed. "I guess when you move, the water passing through the shell makes a noise!" said Ariel.

"Shh, Princess, don't talk so loud. I have a headache! I will see you at the concert tonight." And Sebastian hobbled off, holding one claw to the side of his head. Before long, Sebastian came upon a beautiful, coiled snail shell. "This is more like it!" he said, wiggling into the shell. "Okay, ladies, come and get me!" he shouted. Sebastian began to strut and fell flat on his face!

"This is just a bit too tight!" he gasped, and squeeeezed himself out of the shell. "It won't do at all!"

Just then Alana and her turtle swam by. The turtle snatched up the shell, played with it for a moment, then crunched into it, shattering it to bits.

Sebastian was relieved indeed that he was no longer wearing the shell. He waved to Alana and the turtle and on he went.

Sebastian peered behind seaweed and under rocks, looking for a shell overcoat to wear to the concert that night. Then, almost hidden from sight, he spied something red and purple with bright yellow dots.

"Perfect!" Sebastian cried happily, and he pulled the large shell over his head.

"Very distinctive," he said, and twirled around. "No noise and quite a comfortable fit."

Sebastian smiled. He danced a little jig. He pretended to tip his hat. He bowed. He might have gone on like that for quite a while if he hadn't heard a noise behind him. He turned and saw Aquata, Arista, Andrina, Attina, and Adella covering their mouths with their hands as they howled with laughter.

"And just what is so funny?" Sebastian demanded, trying to hide his embarrassment at having been caught admiring himself.

"Sebastian," said Andrina, as gently as she could, "don't you think that overcoat is a bit too, well, *showy?*"

"The show!" cried Sebastian, "I must get to rehearsal!" He jumped out of the shell and began to hurry off. He looked back at the princesses.

"Ah...thank you," he said curtly, and was off.

"I guess I will have to conduct without an overcoat at all," said Sebastian. "There is just no more time to look for a new one and my old ones simply won't do."

At the end of the performance that night, everyone stood and clapped and clapped. King Triton made a special announcement.

"Sebastian, for all your excellent new music," he said, "I present you with this small token of my esteem." King Triton handed Sebastian a beautifully wrapped box. Inside was a brand-new, golden shell overcoat.

"Your Majesty!" Sebastian gasped. "How did you know that this is absolutely the very thing that I wanted most?" And while Sebastian tried on his new shell, which fit him just perfectly, seven little mermaids exchanged a pleasant wink with their father.

URSULA'S REVENGE

Under the sea there were ripples of excitement as the kingdom prepared to celebrate its biggest holiday. It was the anniversary of the day that King Triton had freed the kingdom from Ursula the Sea Witch. Everyone eagerly awaited the festivities that would mark this most special of days. Everyone, that is, except Ursula and her slimy eels, Flotsam and Jetsam.

Flotsam and Jetsam leaned over the crystal ball. "Hissss," they both said together.

"I'll win back the kingdom someday, and when I do, we'll just see how happy they'll all be then!" Ursula vowed. "But in the meantime, I've got to find a way to *really* make this a day to remember!"

Ursula looked in the crystal ball. She saw extra guards posted around the kingdom.

"They must be waiting for me to try something," said Ursula. "Disappoint them, I won't!" Quickly, she flipped through her *Book of Spells*. She stopped and read one page carefully.

"That's it!" she shrieked. "Why send only one Ursula to ruin things if you can send one hundred? Ursula, old girl, you've still got it!" Ursula rubbed her hands together gleefully and quickly began to mix a magic potion.

"Barnacle flakes, one squid tentacle, jellyfish venom," Ursula muttered as she dropped the ingredients into the pot. "One shark tooth, and—this has to be just right—a dash of barracuda juice!"

Smoky clouds began to billow from the pot. Black bubbles rose and burst. Ursula chuckled. She dipped her ladle into the pot and gulped

down the mixture. When she began to chuckle again, black bubbles rose out of her mouth. Inside each one was a tiny Ursula!

One hundred little black bubbles in all came out of Ursula's mouth. One hundred little Ursulas floated high above the sea's floor. The bubbles rolled out of the cave, off toward the kingdom.

"Hurry, my darlings!" Ursula cried. "Your bubbles will open for only a few minutes, so you must already be in the kingdom, ready to pinch, pilfer, and do whatever you can to ruin this sappy celebration! I know you can do it! Make me proud!"

Ursula waved to the bubbles as they danced off, rising higher and higher in the water.

One hundred bubbles floated right past the palace guards, high above their heads. The guards were peering anxiously into the distance, on the lookout for one big Ursula. They never thought to turn their eyes upward.

Ursula's spell seemed to be working perfectly. The bubbles burst inside the kingdom, as planned. One hundred tiny Ursulas giggled wickedly and set out to make as much mischief as they could in a hurry.

But just as they spread out to rip down decorations, overturn tables of food, pull merpeople's hair, and do many other equally nasty things, the annual beauty contest was announced. Each little Ursula immediately decided to enter the pageant. Back in her cave, Ursula watched through her crystal ball as her hundred little selves abandoned her plan.

"No! You vain little fools!" she cried as she pulled her hair. Ursula leaned closer as a trumpet blast signaled the beginning of the event. One of King Triton's heralds swished forward, cleared his throat, and announced:

"Ladies and gentlemen! I am honored to present the most beautiful and talented creatures under the sea!"

One by one the loveliest creatures in the kingdom came down the swimway. Each of King Triton's daughters performed well and never looked more beautiful. The judges exchanged glances. It would be difficult to pick just one winner.

Then, all of a sudden, one hundred little Ursulas, each one jealous of ninety-nine others, came down the swimway, kicking and screaming at each other. They pulled each other's hair. They kicked sand. They called each other terrible names.

All the mermaids and mermen crowded around as the fight raged on and on. No one knew what to do. Then a strange thing began to happen. Shiny black bubbles formed around each of the little Ursulas. They floated up past the castle, higher and higher. All the merpeople heard one hundred angry shrieks. Then the miniature witches floated away.

Ursula stopped looking into the crystal ball. She sat back and groaned. The one hundred black bubbles bobbed back into her cave. Ursula waited for them to vanish, but when the bubbles popped again, the little Ursulas inside did not disappear. Instead they kept on fighting.

"I must have used too much barracuda juice!" screamed the original Ursula. "What a day to remember this turned out to be after all!" she shrieked, and ran off to find her book of antidotes.

Ursula's Fury

That little brat!
That awful child!
I hear her voice
And just go wild!

To think that *she's*
So young and rich!
While look at me—
An old Sea Witch!

The way I'm treated
Is a sin!
But I'll fix her,
I'll do her in!

Oh, I love it!
I can't wait!
To make a poison
Of my hate!

MARLON'S
AMAZING DISCOVERY

One day Ariel, Flounder, and Ariel's cousin Marlon decided to play hide-and-seek in an old sunken ship half-buried in the ocean floor. Flounder was "It," so Ariel and Marlon swam quickly through the rotting planks looking for good places to hide.

Marlon went to the front of the ship and was about to hide in a big steamer trunk, when he noticed a strange shape in the murky water. He reached over and pulled away some seaweed that covered the object.

"Ariel, Flounder, come take a look at this!" Marlon shouted excitedly.

"What is it?" Ariel asked. Marlon pointed to his discovery.

"Oh!" Ariel and Flounder cried together. For there, carved in the prow of the ship, was the face of a young girl.

"It's a human figure, carved out of wood," said Ariel, tugging away more of the seaweed. "She's part of the ship."

Indeed, the wooden girl leaned forward from the front end of the ship. Her arms were crossed against her body, and her carved hair flowed back from her face.

"Let's clean her up," said Ariel. "Then we'll be able to see what she really looks like." And with that, she began to rub away the barnacles and moss that covered the girl's face and dress.

Every day Ariel returned to the ship to clean up the wooden girl. On the first day, Marlon went with her and helped Ariel brush the mud from the girl's eyes. On the second day, Flounder watched as Ariel scraped mud from the girl's hair. On the third day, Ariel scrubbed moss from her dress. On the fourth day, the girl was missing! Ariel gasped and looked

around wildly. Where could she be?

"Up here!" called a voice.

Ariel looked up. There, perched on the ship's mast, was a beautiful mermaid.

"Don't you recognize me?" the mermaid asked.

Ariel looked at the mermaid closely. Why, she looked just like the wooden girl from the ship!

"Let me explain," said the mermaid. "My name is Kate. I was a human girl. My father was a sea captain, and I loved to sail with him. One day I saw a handsome merman swimming in the water and I fell in love with him instantly. I could not stop thinking of him and longed to be by his side. It all seemed hopeless until a strange creature came to see me. Her name was Ursula."

"The Sea Witch!" Ariel cried. "She usually makes mischief *under* the sea. She must have been awfully bored below to work her evil on the surface."

"I don't know if she was bored," said Kate, "but I do know she was mean! She told me she knew of a magic spell that would change me into a mermaid three days after I saw my merman again. I wanted so badly to be with him that I didn't think to ask what the details were. I quickly agreed, and with an evil laugh Ursula changed me into a figure on the prow of my father's ship. She told me that this way I could keep a constant watch for my love."

"Ursula is usually more than just mean," said Ariel. "She usually wants something, too."

"Well, I never found out what it was," said Kate, "because that very night, there was a terrible storm that sank the ship."

"And you've been stuck here ever since," added Ariel.

"That's right," said Kate. Then she swam a little and stretched her arms over her head. "But thanks to you, I can see again! You brushed the mud away from my eyes."

"And you're a mermaid!" said Ariel excitedly. "You must have seen your merman!"

"I have," said Kate. "He's your cousin Marlon!" She gave Ariel a hug. "Will you take me to him?"

"Of course!" Ariel said, laughing. "But you must promise to tell me what it was like to be a human and to live on land."

"It's a deal," said Kate. "As soon as I've seen Marlon, I'll be happy to tell you anything you'd like to know."

Ariel couldn't wait to hear Kate's stories about life on land. She thought to herself that she could not imagine ever being so much in love that she would stoop to asking Ursula for help. But Kate could not possibly have known about Ursula and her evil tricks. And everything had turned out okay, or would, Ariel thought, as soon as Marlon saw the beautiful mermaid who longed to be with him. Ariel returned Kate's hug, and then the two mermaids linked arms and swam off together.

A DAY IN THE
LIFE OF A MERMAID

"Just look at that girl," Sebastian said, "loafing about, daydreaming. Ariel, sometimes I think you've got seagrass for brains."

Ariel didn't even look up. She was busy doodling in the sand. She was thinking about humans. Humans had created so many wonderful things that she had found on the ocean floor. And humans lived on the surface. Ariel closed her eyes and began to remember all the stories she had heard from Kate, Scuttle, and the others about those strange creatures with legs instead of fins.

"Waah! Waah! Waaaaah!"

The crying interrupted Ariel's thoughts. She saw a little shrimp crying.

"What's the matter?" she asked. "Are you lost?"

The tiny shrimp nodded.

"Waah! Waah! Waah!"

"Okay, okay," Ariel said, lifting him up. "Don't you belong at Crayfish School?" She carried the little fellow carefully to the school, where he happily joined the other little shrimps.

Ariel watched as the little shrimps played, but soon she was thinking about life on land again. She wondered if humans went to school.

"Hey, Ariel! Want to dance?"

Ariel looked over her shoulder. There was Briny, with his eight left feet! Ariel groaned to herself. Briny was such a bad dancer! If only he knew that, but Ariel would never tell him. She just couldn't hurt his feelings.

"Please, Ariel?" Briny begged. "You can use some of my feet."

Sighing, Ariel held out her arms and let Briny lead her around. He twirled her and lifted her up until she got very dizzy.

"I think we'd better stop now," she said, after he had dipped her for the fifth time.

"Oh, sure, sure. Thanks a lot, Ariel. With a little practice you'll probably be a pretty good dancer someday," he said, waving good-bye with all eight legs.

Ariel was wondering what it would be like to dance with a human, when she heard a soft mewing nearby.

"What in the great green ocean," Ariel said. She looked around. There was her sister's pet catfish, Fin-Fin, all tangled up in a coral bed.

"How did you ever get out here?" she said as she carefully pulled Fin-Fin out of the coral bed. "Attina doesn't like for you to get out of the castle." The catfish purred in Ariel's arms, and they swam back to the castle side by side.

As soon as Ariel arrived at the castle, Adella whisked her away to their bedroom.

"Ariel," she said excitedly. "I need to ask you a favor. Will you lend me your mother-of-pearl comb? I've got a big date tonight, and it will look divine in my hair."

Ariel found the comb in her jewel box, but of course Adella wanted her to arrange her hair for her as well.

"You're so clever with hair, Ariel," Adella said, patting her hair in place. "It's a shame you just let yours go." Then she blew Ariel a kiss and floated out the door.

"Hmmm," Ariel thought, peering at her reflection. She piled all her hair on top of her head. Then she let it drop again. "I wonder if humans wear their hair up or down."

She was about to try a braid when Arista burst in.

"Ariel, come quickly!" Arista pleaded. "It's Mackey's day off and someone left the stable door open. Foamy's loose!"

Ariel swam out to the stables, where she and Arista finally cornered Foamy and led him back to his stall.

"Thanks for your help," Arista said as she closed the stable door tightly.

"Do you think humans have any animals like seahorses?" Ariel wondered.

"Are you kidding?" Arista scoffed. "They have to get around on their ugly old legs."

"I don't think legs are ugly at all," said Ariel. "Haven't you ever thought about what it must be like to walk on land?"

"Ariel!" said Arista, shocked. "Why would you want to walk on land when you can swim in the ocean?"

Ariel could not give her sister a simple answer so she swam off without answering and went back to her doodles. She began to daydream about walking on land. Everyone would marvel at how graceful she was and beg her to dance, and, and—

But Ariel never finished her thought. She was interrupted by Sebastian.

"Look at that girl," he complained. "She hasn't moved from that spot all day."

Ariel just looked at Sebastian and smiled.

Ariel's Dream

I've always tried so hard to be
What everyone expects of me.
But lately I've a nagging thought
That goes against all I've been taught.

The world above seems bright and wide,
And yet, down here is where we hide.
There's something that just isn't right
With living here without sunlight.

For now I'll dream among the waves
And keep collections in my caves.
I know there has to be a way
That I can live on land one day.